THE LIBRARY DOORS

Toni Buzzeo

Pictures by
Nadine Bernard Westcott

UpstartBooks

Fort Atkinson, Wisconsin
www.upstartbooks.com

To Catherine and the students of Longfellow School,
where the library doors are always swinging.
—T. B.

To Will and Kendall,
Love, Deanie
—N. B. W.

Published by UpstartBooks
W5527 State Road 106
P.O. Box 800
Fort Atkinson, Wisconsin 53538-0800
1-800-448-4887

Text © 2008 by Toni Buzzeo
Illustrations © 2008 by Nadine Bernard Westcott

The library doors swing
OPEN AND SHUT,
OPEN AND SHUT,
OPEN AND SHUT.
The library doors swing
OPEN AND SHUT
All through the day!

The children in our school can
COME AND GO,
COME AND GO,
COME AND GO.
The children in our school can
COME AND GO
All through the day!

The kids at the doors say,
SHHH, SHHH, SHHH,
SHHH, SHHH, SHHH,
SHHH, SHHH, SHHH.
The kids at the doors say,
SHHH, SHHH, SHHH
All through the day!

Our library teacher says
COME, LET'S TALK,
COME, LET'S TALK,
COME, LET'S TALK.
Our library teacher says
COME, LET'S TALK,
But whisper if you can.

We sit on the rug to
HEAR A TALE,
HEAR A TALE,
HEAR A TALE.
We sit on the rug to
HEAR A TALE
All through the day!

The catalog screen lists
AUTHORS WE LIKE,
TITLES WE KNOW,
SUBJECTS WE WANT.
The catalog screen lists
BOOKS WE LOVE
All through the day!

Help

We head to the shelves to
LOOK FOR BOOKS,
LOOK FOR BOOKS,
LOOK FOR BOOKS.
We head to the shelves to
LOOK FOR BOOKS
All through the day!

PICTURE BOOKS

N-Q

R-T

U-Z

The markers in the shelves will
HOLD OUR SPOTS,
HOLD OUR SPOTS,
HOLD OUR SPOTS.
The markers in the shelves will
HOLD OUR SPOTS
All through the day!

We open the covers to
READ, READ, READ,
READ, READ, READ,
READ, READ, READ.
We open the covers to
READ, READ, READ
All through the day!

The keys on computers go
TICKETY TICK,
TICKETY TICK,
TICKETY TICK.
The keys on computers go
TICKETY TICK
All through the day!

We search online for
TOWNS AND STATES,
FAMOUS FOLKS,
ANIMALS.
We search online for
FACTS WE NEED
All through the day!

The library books check
IN AND OUT,
IN AND OUT,
IN AND OUT.
The library books check
IN AND OUT
All through the day!

Our time is up so we
WAVE GOODBYE,
WAVE GOODBYE,
WAVE GOODBYE.
Our time is up so we
WAVE GOODBYE
To our librarian.

She makes us promise we'll
COME AGAIN,
COME AGAIN,
COME AGAIN.
She makes us promise we'll
COME AGAIN
Tomorrow if we can.

We're sad to leave but
WE'LL BE BACK,
WE'LL BE BACK,
WE'LL BE BACK.
We're sad to leave but
WE'LL BE BACK
All through the year!